COOL CATS COUNTING

by Sherry Shahan
Illustrated by Paula Barragán

AUGUST HOUSE
LittleFolk

August House LittleFolk
LITTLE ROCK

One goat

    hotsy solo

        twanger-toes.

        GO, MAN, GO!

UNA CHIVA

Two dogs
hip-hop
bop-romp.
HO, DADDY-O!

DOS PERROS

Three geese
flappin' feet
flutter beat.
WOOO-WEEE!

3

TRES GANSOS

Four cows
twist-and-shout
dip-and-bow.
HOLY COW!

CUATRO VACAS

Five donkeys

doodle-do

yahoo toot.

HOOF IT, MAN!

5

CINCO BURROS

Six pigs

flip-flop-drop

S

L

O

P

!

SLICK AS A LICK!

SEIS CERDOS

7

Seven rabbits
jump-and-jive
slappin' high-five.
ZIPPETY-DO-RAH!

SIETE CONEJOS

Eight rats
Spin and snap
Rat-a-tat-tat
HIGH JINKS!

OCHO RATAS

Nine chickens
struttin' stuff
shakin' it up.
LICKETY-SPLIT!
NUEVE GALLINAS

Ten cats

hep cats

cuttin' a rug.

JITTERBUG!

DIEZ GATOS

Snazzy-jazzy animals
boogie all day

woogie all night.
BOP CITY
BIRD LAND

ROYAL ROOST

PRONUNCIATION

NUMBERS

Una (UU-nah)

Dos (dohs)

Tres (trehs)

Cuatro (K'WAH-troh)

Cinco (SINK-koh)

Seis (SAY-ees)

Siete (S'YEH-tay)

Ocho (OH-choh)

Nueve (Nu-WAY-bay)

Diez (dee-YEHS)

ANIMALS

Burros (BUR-ros)

Cerdos (SAIR-dohs)

Chivos (CHEE-bohs)

Conejos (ko-NAY-hos)

Gallinas (gah-YEE-nahs)

Gansos (GAHN-sohs)

Gatos (GAH-tohs)

Perros (PEH-rrohs)

Ratas (RRAH-tahs)

Vacas (BAH-kahs)

For my dear friend, Corey Rubbo XO — S.S.

A Maio, Bruno y Ana por su gran ayuda — P.B.

Text copyright © 2005 by Sherry Shahan.
Illustrations copyright © 2005 by Paula Barragán.
All rights reserved. This book, or parts thereof, may not be reproduced
in any form without permission.

Published 2005 by August House LittleFolk,
P.O. Box 3223, Little Rock, Arkansas 72203
501-372-5450
http://www.augusthouse.com

Book design by Mina Greenstein
Manufactured in Korea
10 9 8 7 6 5 4 3 2 1   HC

LIBRARY OF CONGRESS CATALOGING-IN-PUBLIC
Shahan, Sherry.
Cool cats counting / Sherry Shahan ; illust
          p.   cm.
1. Counting—Juvenile literature. I. Ba
QA113.S5 2005
513.2'11—dc22

The paper used in this publicati
the American National Standard
of Paper for Printed Library Mater